SHERLOCK HOLMES

at quarter to twelve
learn what
maybe

THE REIGATE SQUIRES

SIR ARTHUR CONAN DOYLE

Sweet Cherry
PUBLISHING

THE
SHERLOCK
HOLMES

CHILDREN'S COLLECTION

SHADOWS, SECRETS AND STOLEN TREASURE

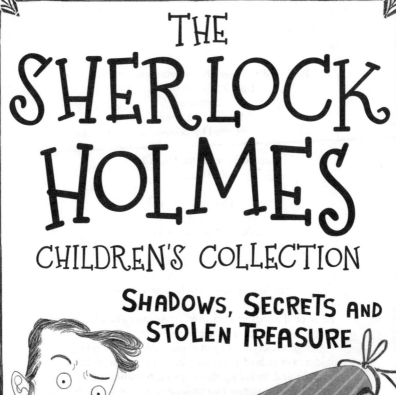

Published by Sweet Cherry Publishing Limited
Unit 36, Vulcan House,
Vulcan Road,
Leicester, LE5 3EF
United Kingdom

First published in the UK in 2019
2019 edition

2 4 6 8 10 9 7 5 3 1

ISBN: 978-1-78226-414-9

Sherlock Holmes: The Reigate Squires

Based on the original story from Sir Arthur Conan Doyle,
adapted by Stephanie Baudet.

Cover Design by Arianna Bellucci and Rhiannon Izard
Illustrations by Arianna Bellucci

www.sweetcherrypublishing.com

Printed in India
I.IPP001

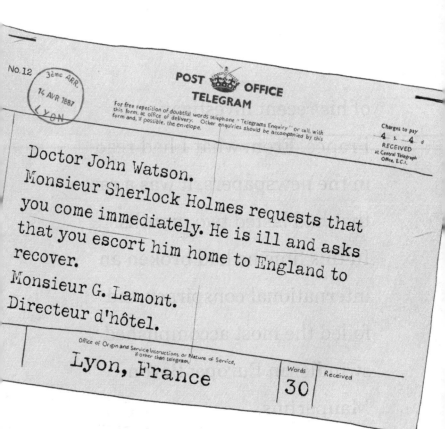

No. 12
3ème ARR.
14 AVR 1887
LYON

Charges to pay
4 s. 4 d
RECEIVED
at Central Telegraph
Office, E.C.1.

POST OFFICE TELEGRAM

For free repetition of doubtful words telephone "Telegrams Enquiry" or call, with this form, at office of delivery. Other enquiries should be accompanied by this form and, if possible, the envelope.

Doctor John Watson.
Monsieur Sherlock Holmes requests that you come immediately. He is ill and asks that you escort him home to England to recover.
Monsieur G. Lamont.
Directeur d'hôtel.

Office of Origin and Service Instructions or Nature of Service, if other than telegram.

Lyon, France

Words 30 | Received

It was on the fourteenth of April 1887 that I received a telegram from Lyon with the news that Sherlock Holmes had become ill under the strain of his recent investigation in France. From what I had read in the newspapers, it was a case that had lasted two months. In this time he had broken an international conspiracy and foiled the most accomplished swindler in Europe: Baron Maupertuis.

wo month gation led arrest of Maupertuis ight as the national wned detective lock Holmes eeded where e national ce forces had ed. The baron's uence over

the Netherland-Sumatra Company had long caused concern in financial circles. Yesterday's discoveries revealed the swindling baron's plot would have led to an economic collapse of a level unseen since the Panic of 1866. The arrest

took place after a tense six-hour standoff. Holmes finally obtained access to the baron's quarters disguised as his close ally. Officials from several European governments have come forward to congratulate the detective.

For all those weeks he had worked fifteen hours a day and had more than once kept at his task for five days at a time.

Within twenty-four hours I was by Holmes' side at the hotel. Even *his* strong health had broken down under the strain. He was in the deepest depression, despite the fact that Europe was ringing with his name and his room was ankle-deep in telegrams of congratulations.

Even the knowledge that he had succeeded where the police of three countries had failed had evidently not been enough to raise his spirits. I had been worried when I'd received the urgent telegram, but he was very pleased to see me and seemed to improve from the moment I arrived. His eyes lit up as I entered the room and he sat up and

reached out to grasp my hand.

'Watson, my dear fellow. It is good of you to come.'

He looked pale and exhausted but I felt a wave of relief as I noticed a hint of the old Holmes in his expression.

I soon busied myself with the task of making arrangements for our voyage to England and three days later we were back in Baker Street.

My old friend Colonel Hayter, who had been a patient of mine in Afghanistan, had often asked me to visit him in Reigate. He had recently asked if Holmes would like to come with me. Sensing my hesitation, he assured me that he would be very welcome. I thought that a week of spring sunshine in the country would help Holmes' recovery. It would suit me too,

Reigate

A nice enough town, although with little of note other than the demolished castle. Has several large houses that may prove attractive to burglars who are not looking for great reward. A small local police force that is likely to be ineffective.

since my medical practice had been especially busy recently.

However, Holmes – as I expected – insisted that he could look after himself. I did not need his detective skills to see this was not the case, and after several attempts I eventually succeeded in convincing him to accept the colonel's invitation. It was only when I made it clear that the colonel lived alone and would allow Holmes to relax and do as he pleased that he finally gave in.

A week later we were in the Surrey countryside. Hayter was a fine soldier who had seen much of the world. He and Holmes found they had much in common as they talked about their travels.

On the evening of our arrival we were sitting in the colonel's gun room after dinner. Holmes lay stretched out upon the sofa,

while Hayter and I looked at his collection of Eastern weapons.

'By the way,' he said suddenly, 'I think I'll take one of these pistols upstairs with me in case we have an alarm.'

'An alarm?' I said.

'Yes, we've had a scare in these parts lately. Old Acton, who is a local wealthy businessman, had his house broken into last Monday. No great damage done, but the burglars haven't yet been caught.'

'No clue?' asked Holmes, casting a glance at the colonel.

I frowned, hoping he wouldn't get drawn in.

'None as yet. But it's a petty crime, which must seem too small for your attention,

Mr Holmes, after this great international affair.'

Holmes waved away the compliment, although I noticed by his smile that it had pleased him. 'Was there anything interesting about it?'

The colonel shook his head. 'The thieves ransacked the library but got very little. The whole place was turned upside down but all that was taken was an old book, two silver candlesticks, an ivory

paperweight, a small oak
barometer and a ball
of string.'

'What an extraordinary
assortment!' I exclaimed.

'Oh, the burglars
must have grabbed
everything they
could get.'

Holmes grunted
from the sofa.

'The county police
ought to make something
of that,' he said. 'Why,

surely it is obvious that–'

I held up a warning finger. 'You are here for rest, my dear fellow. For heaven's sake, don't get started on a new case when your nerves are all in shreds.'

Holmes shrugged, with a glance of amused resignation at the colonel. He just couldn't resist a mystery, and I was going to have a problem making him rest.

As it turned out, all my advice as a doctor was wasted, for the following morning the puzzle became impossible to ignore.

We were at breakfast when the colonel's butler rushed in without his usual dignified manner.

'Have you heard the news, sir?' he gasped. 'At the Cunninghams', sir!'

'Burglary?' cried the colonel, with his coffee cup still in mid-air.

'Murder!'

The colonel whistled. 'By Jove!' he said. 'Who's killed? The squire or his son?'

'Neither, sir. It was William, the coachman. Shot through the heart, sir, and never spoke again.'

'Who shot him, then?'

'The burglar, sir. He got clean away. He'd just broke in at the pantry window, I believe, when William came on him and met his end saving his master's property.'

'What time?'

'It was last night, sir, around twelve.'

'Ah, then we'll go over there later,' said the colonel, coolly settling down to his breakfast again. 'It's a bad business,' he added when the butler had gone. 'He's a very decent man, is old Cunningham, and may be glad of a word of sympathy. He'll be cut up about this. The man worked for him for years and was a good employee. It's evidently the same villains who broke into Acton's.'

'And stole that very strange collection,' said Holmes, thoughtfully.

'Precisely.'

'Hmm,' said Holmes. 'It may prove to be the simplest matter in the world, but all the same, at first glance this is just a little curious, is it not? A gang of burglars robbing two houses

in the same district within a few days. You would think that they would go further afield to somewhere busier and more populated. When you spoke last night of taking precautions, I remember thinking that this was probably the last place in England to which thieves would turn their attention – which shows that I still have much to learn.'

'It's sure to be someone local,' said the colonel. 'In which case,

Acton's and Cunningham's are just the places they would go for, since they are the largest houses about here.'

'And richest?'

'Well, they ought to be, but they've had a court case for some years that has cost them both a lot of money, I should imagine. Old Acton has some claim on half of Cunningham's estate, and the lawyers have been fighting the case for a long time.'

'If it's a local villain there

should not be much difficulty in finding him,' said Holmes with a yawn. He sensed what I was about to say and glanced at me with a smile. 'All right, Watson. I don't intend to meddle.'

I was not sure I believed him, but my thoughts were interrupted by a knock at the front door and voices in the hall.

The butler entered, followed by a smart, keen-faced young fellow. 'Inspector Forrester, sir,' he announced.

I looked at the official with interest as he stepped into the room.

'Good morning, Colonel,' he said. 'I hope I don't intrude, but I hear that Mr Sherlock Holmes of Baker Street is here.'

The colonel waved towards my friend and the inspector bowed.

'We thought that perhaps you would care to help, Mr Holmes.'

'The fates are against you, Watson,' said Holmes, looking at me and laughing. He turned back to the policeman. 'We were chatting about the matter when you came in, Inspector. Perhaps you can let us have a few details.'

As he leaned back in his chair in the familiar attitude, I knew it was hopeless. My idea of a rest in the country had failed.

'We had no clue in the Acton

affair,' said the inspector, taking a seat facing Holmes. 'But we have plenty to go on this time, and there's no doubt it was the same person in each case. The man was seen.'

'Ah!'

'Yes, sir. But he was off like a deer after firing the shot that killed poor William Kirwan, the coachman. Mr Cunningham saw him from the bedroom window, and his son saw him from the back corridor. It was quarter to twelve when the alarm was raised. Mr Cunningham had just got into bed, and Mr Alec was in his dressing room. They both heard William calling for help, and Mr Alec ran down to see what the matter was.

'The back door was open and, as he came to the foot of the stairs, he saw two men wrestling together outside. One of them fired a shot, the other dropped to the ground, and the murderer rushed across the garden and over the hedge.'

He paused and took a breath
to continue the story. I glanced
at Holmes with concern,
searching for any signs of strain.
But there were none. His eyes
were alive and
sparkling as he
waited for more,
his fingers steepled
and tapping
against his mouth
thoughtfully.

The inspector continued. 'Mr Cunningham, looking out of his bedroom, saw the fellow as he reached the road, but lost sight of him at once. Mr Alec stopped to see if he could help the dying man, and so the villain got away. We have no way of identifying him other than the fact that he was dressed in dark clothes, but we are making enquiries and if he is a stranger we shall soon find him.'

'What was this William doing

there? Did he say anything before he died?'

The inspector shook his head. 'Not a word. He lives at the lodge with his mother, and as he was a very faithful fellow we imagine that he walked up to the house to see that everything was all right. Of course, this Acton business has put everyone on their guard. The robber must have just burst open the door – the lock has been forced – when William came upon him.'

'Did William say anything to his mother before going out?'

'She is very old and deaf, and we can get no information from her. The shock has caused her to suffer an attack of brain-fever and made her confused.'

As I wondered if any doctors in the area had been to help the unfortunate lady, I became aware that the inspector was still talking. Sheepishly I returned my attention to him.

'There is one very important

clue, however. Look at this!'

He took a small piece of torn paper from a notebook and spread it out on his knee.

'This was found between the finger and thumb of the dead man. It appears to be a fragment torn from a larger sheet. You will see that the hour mentioned on it is the very time at which the poor fellow met his fate. You see, the murderer may have torn the rest of the sheet from his victim, or William might have taken this fragment from the murderer. It reads almost as though it were an appointment.'

Holmes took up the scrap of paper and I glanced over his shoulder to read it.

at quarter to twelve
learn what
maybe

'Assuming that it is an appointment,' went on the inspector, 'it is, of course, possible that this William Kirwan may have been in league with the thief, even though he was thought to be an honest man. He may have met him there and helped him break in the door before they had an argument.'

'This writing is of great interest,' said Holmes, who had been examining it closely.

'This is much more complicated than I thought.' He rested his head on his hands, while the inspector smiled at the effect his case was having upon the famous London detective.

Finally Holmes looked up. 'Your last remark that the burglar and Kirwan may have been in this together is an ingenious and not impossible idea. But this writing opens up ...' He bowed his head and remained for some minutes in deepest thought. When he raised his face again I was surprised to see that his cheeks were tinged with colour and his eyes as bright as before his illness. He sprang to his feet with all his old energy.

'I'll tell you what,' he said. 'I should like to have a quiet little glance at the details of this case. There is something in it that fascinates me enormously. If you will permit me, Colonel, I will leave my friend Watson with you, and I will go to the police station with the inspector to test the truth of one or two ideas of mine. I will be with you again in half an hour.'

An hour and a half went by before the inspector returned alone.

'Mr Holmes is walking up and down in a field outside,' he said. 'He wants all four of us to go up to the house together.'

'To Mr Cunningham's?' asked the colonel.

'Yes, sir.'

'What for?'

The inspector shrugged. 'I don't quite know, sir. Between ourselves, I don't think Mr Holmes has quite got over his illness yet. He's been behaving very oddly, and he is very excited.'

'I don't think you need alarm yourself,' I said. 'I have usually found that there was method in his madness.'

'Some folk might say there was madness in his method,' muttered the inspector. 'But he's anxious to start, Colonel, so we had best go out if you are ready.'

We found Holmes pacing up and down in the field, his chin sunk upon his chest and his hands thrust into his trouser pockets.

'This matter becomes more and more interesting,' he said. 'Watson, your country trip has been a distinct success. I have had a charming morning.'

I smiled. I was pleased to see how well he looked, but he was only human, and his body and mind needed rest to heal.

I had begun to regret my plan to get him away to the country. He was not resting, and I feared a relapse.

'You have been up to the scene of the crime, I understand,' said the colonel.

'Yes. The inspector and I have made quite a little exploration together.'

'Any success?'

'Well, we have seen some very interesting things. I'll tell you what we did as we walk. First of all, we saw the body of the unfortunate man. He certainly died from a gunshot wound as reported.'

'Had you doubted it then?'

'Oh, it is good practice to test everything. Our inspection was not wasted. We then had an interview with Mr Cunningham and his son, who were able to point out the exact spot where the murderer broke through the garden hedge as he got away. That was of great interest.'

'Of course.'

'Then we went to see the poor fellow's mother. We could get no information from her, however, as she is very old and feeble.'

'And what is the result of your investigations?'

'The certainty that the crime is a very odd one. Perhaps our visit now may make it clearer. I think we are both agreed, Inspector, that the fragment of paper in the dead man's hand is of extreme importance. It bears

the hour of
his death.'

'It should
give us a clue,
Mr Holmes.'

'It *does* give
a clue. Whoever
wrote that note was
the man who got Mr
William Kirwan out
of his bed at that hour. But
where is the rest of that sheet
of paper?'

'I examined the ground

*at quarter to twelve
learn what
maybe*

carefully in the hope of finding it,' said the inspector.

'It was torn out of the dead man's hand. Why was someone so anxious to get it? Because it proved that he was guilty. And what would he do with it? Thrust it into his pocket most likely, never noticing that a corner of it had been left in the grip of the dead man. If we could get the rest of that sheet we would go a long way to solving the mystery.'

'Yes, but how can we get at the criminal's pocket before we catch the criminal?'

'Well well, it was worth thinking over. Then there is another obvious point. The note was sent to William. The man who wrote it could not have taken it; otherwise, of course, he could have told William the message himself. Who brought the note then? Or did it come through the post?'

'I have made enquiries,' said

the inspector. 'William received a letter by the afternoon post yesterday and destroyed the envelope.'

'Excellent!' cried Holmes, clapping the inspector on the back. 'You've seen the postman! It is a pleasure to work with you. Well, here is the lodge, and if you will come in, Colonel, I will show you the scene of the crime.'

We passed the pretty cottage where the murdered man had lived and walked up an oak-lined avenue to the elegant manor house. Holmes and the inspector led us round to the side gate, which was separated from the hedge that lined the road by a stretch of garden.

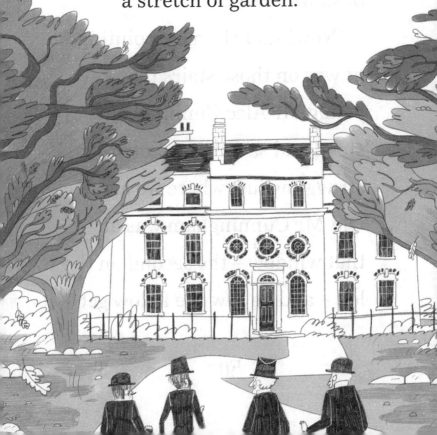

A constable was standing at the back door and he opened it as we approached, revealing a short corridor with a door to the kitchen on one side and a flight of stairs ahead.

'Now,' said Holmes, pointing, 'it was on those stairs that young Mr Alec Cunningham stood and saw the two men struggling just where we are. Old Mr Cunningham was at that window – the second on the left – and he saw the fellow get away just to the left of that bush. So did the son. They are both sure of it. Then Mr Alec ran out and knelt beside the wounded man. The ground is very hard, you see, so there are no marks to guide us.'

As he spoke, two men came down the garden path from round the corner of the house. One was an elderly man with a strong, heavily-lined, heavy-eyed face. The other was a dashing young fellow, whose bright smiling expression and showy clothes were in strange contrast to the sad events that had brought us here.

'Still at it then?' he said to Holmes. 'I thought you Londoners were never at fault. You don't seem to be very quick.'

'Ah, you must give us a little time,' said Holmes, good-naturedly.

'You'll want it,' said young Alec Cunningham, still smiling. 'I don't see that we have any clue at all.'

'There's only one,' answered the inspector. 'We thought that if we could only find– Good heavens, Mr Holmes. What is the matter?'

My poor friend's face had suddenly taken on a dreadful expression. His eyes rolled upwards, his features writhed in agony and, with a groan, he dropped on his face on the ground.

Horrified at the seriousness of the attack, I dropped to my knees beside him. So he was vulnerable after all. 'Let's get him inside quickly,' I said.

We carried him into the kitchen where he lay back in a large chair, breathing heavily for a few minutes. Finally he looked at us, shamefaced at his weakness, and got to his feet.

'Watson will tell you that I have only just recovered from a serious illness,' he explained. 'I am liable to these sudden nervous attacks.'

I nodded my agreement.

'Shall I send you home in my carriage?' asked Old Cunningham.

'Well, since I am here, there is one point on which I should like to feel sure. We can very easily check it.'

'What is it?'

'Well, it seems to me it's possible that poor William arrived after, and not before, the burglar entered the house. You appear to take it for granted

that, although the door was
forced, the robber never actually
got in the house.'

'I think that's quite obvious,'
said Mr Cunningham, gravely.
'My son Alec had not yet gone to
bed, and he would certainly have
heard someone moving about.'

'Where was he sitting?'

'I was sitting in my dressing
room,' said Alec.

'Which window is that?'

'The last on the left, next to my
father's room.'

'Both of your lamps were lit, of course?'

'Of course.'

'There are some very strange points here,' said Holmes, smiling. 'Is it not odd that a burglar – and one with previous experience – should break into a house when he could see from the lights that the family were still up?'

Inspector Forrester nodded. 'He must have had nerves of steel.'

'Well, of course, if the case

were not such an odd one, we should not have had to ask you for an explanation,' said Mr Alec. 'But as for your idea that the man had robbed the house before William tackled him, I think it is a most absurd notion. Wouldn't we have found the place in a mess and missed the things that he had taken?'

'It depends on what the things were,' said Holmes. 'You must remember that we are dealing with a very peculiar burglar who appears to have a method of his own. Look, for example, at the strange lot of things that he took from Acton's – what was it? – a ball of string, a paperweight, and I don't know what other odds and ends.'

'Well, we are quite in your hands, Mr Holmes,' said Old Cunningham. 'Anything that you or the inspector may suggest will most certainly be done.'

'In the first place,' said Holmes, 'I should like you to offer a reward – the police can take a long time to agree an amount, and these things cannot be done too promptly. I have jotted down the form here, if you would not mind signing it. Fifty pounds is quite enough, I think.'

'I would willingly give five hundred,' said Cunningham,

taking the slip of paper that Holmes handed to him. 'This is not quite correct, however,' he said, glancing over the document.

'I wrote it rather hurriedly,' said Holmes.

Cunningham pointed. 'You see you begin, "At about quarter to one on Tuesday morning an attempt was made," and so on. It was a quarter to twelve, in fact.'

I felt sorry for Holmes at the mistake, for I knew how he would feel about making a slip of any kind. He prided himself on being absolutely correct about any fact, but his recent illness had shaken him, and this one little incident was enough to show me that he was still far from being himself.

He was obviously embarrassed for an instant, while the inspector raised his eyebrows, and Alec Cunningham burst into a laugh. His father took up a pen and corrected the mistake, then handed the paper back to Holmes.

'Get it printed as soon as possible,' he said. 'I think your idea is an excellent one.'

Holmes put the slip of paper carefully away into his wallet. 'And now,' he said, 'it really would be a good thing if we all went over the house together and made certain that this rather odd burglar did not carry anything away with him after all.'

Before entering, Holmes had examined the door, which had been forced. It was obvious that a chisel or strong knife had been thrust in and the lock forced back with it. We could see the marks in the wood where it had been pushed in.

'You don't use bars on the windows then?' asked Holmes.

'We have never found it necessary.'

'You don't keep a dog?'

'We do, but he is chained up on the other side of the house.'

'When do the staff go to bed?'

'About ten o' clock.'

'I understand that William was usually also in bed at that hour?'

'Yes.'

'It is odd that on this particular

night he was up. Now, I would be very glad if you would show us over the house, Mr Cunningham.'

We followed him along a stone-floored passage with kitchens branching away from it, and went up a wooden staircase directly to the first floor of the house. This came out onto a landing opposite a second more decorative staircase that came up from the main hall. Off this landing were the drawing room and several

bedrooms, including those of
Mr Cunningham and his son.

Holmes walked slowly along
the landing, looking carefully at
the architecture of the house. I
could tell from his expression
that he was on a hot scent, and
yet I could not guess where his
reasoning was taking him.

'My good sir,' said Mr
Cunningham impatiently,
'surely this is very unnecessary.
This is my room at the end of
the stairs, and my son's is the

one beyond it. Do you think
it was possible for the thief to
have come up here without
disturbing us?'

'You must
get on a fresh
scent, I think,'
said the son
with a rather
malicious smile.

Holmes ignored
the younger man
and instead
smiled patiently

69

at Mr Cunningham. 'Still, I must ask you to humour me a little further. I would like to see how far the windows of the bedrooms look out on the front of the house. This, I understand, is your son's room.' He pushed open the door at which he had stopped and looked inside. 'And that, I presume, is the dressing room in which he was sitting when the alarm was given. Where does the window of that room look out to?'

He stepped across the bedroom, pushed open the door, and glanced around the other room.

'I hope that you're satisfied now?' said Mr Cunningham, tartly.

'Thank you. I think I have seen all that I wished,' replied Holmes.

'Then, if it is really necessary, we can go into my room.'

'If it is not too much trouble.'

The old man shrugged and led the way into his own room, which was plainly furnished. As

we moved towards the window,
Holmes hung back until he and
I were the last of the group.
Near the foot of the bed stood
a small table. On it was a dish
of oranges and a jug of water.
As we passed it, Holmes, to my
utter astonishment, leaned over
in front of me and deliberately
knocked the whole thing over.
The jug smashed into a thousand
pieces and the fruit rolled to
every corner of the room.

'You've done it now, Watson,'

he said coolly. 'An awful mess you've made on the carpet.'

I stooped to pick up the fruit, feeling a little confused. For some unknown reason my companion wanted me to take the blame, but no doubt he would explain his actions later.

As usual, I would have to be patient. The others came to help and set the table on its legs again.

'Hello, where's he got to?' asked the inspector.

Holmes had disappeared.

'Wait here an instant,' said young Alec Cunningham. 'The fellow has gone mad in my opinion. Come with me, Father, and we will see where he has got to.'

They rushed out of the room leaving the inspector, the colonel and I staring at each other.

'I am inclined to agree with Mr Alec,' said the inspector. 'It may be the effect of his illness, but it seems to me that–'

His words were cut short by a sudden scream of 'Help! Help! Murder!' With a shock, I recognised the voice as that of Holmes and rushed madly from the room and onto the landing.

The cries, which had sunk down into a hoarse shouting, came from the room that we

had visited first. I dashed in,
and on into the dressing room
beyond. The two Cunninghams
were bending over the figure
of Holmes, who was
lying on the floor.

The younger man was clutching Holmes' throat with both hands, while the elder seemed to be twisting one of his wrists.

In an instant, the three of us had torn them away from him, and Holmes staggered to his feet, very pale and greatly exhausted.

'Arrest these men, Inspector,' he gasped.

'On what charge?'

'That of murdering their coachman, William Kirwan.'

The inspector stared about him

in bewilderment. 'Oh, come now, Mr Holmes,' he said at last, 'I'm sure you don't really mean to–'

'Tut, man, look at their faces!' cried Holmes curtly.

I had certainly never seen a plainer look of guilt on a human face. The older man seemed numbed and dazed with a heavy, sullen expression on his face. The son, on the other hand, had dropped all his jaunty, dashing style. Instead the ferocity of a dangerous wild beast gleamed in his dark eyes and distorted his handsome face.

The inspector said nothing but, stepping to the door, he blew his whistle. Two of his constables came at the call.

'I have no alternative, Mr Cunningham,' he said. 'I expect that this will all prove to be an absurd mistake, but you can see that– Ah, drop it!' He struck out with his hand and a revolver, which the younger man was in the act of retrieving from his pocket, clattered down upon the floor.

'Keep that,' said Holmes, putting his foot on it. 'You will find it useful at the trial. But this is what we really wanted.' He held up a little crumpled piece of paper.

'The remainder of the sheet!' cried the inspector.

'Precisely.'

'And where was it?'

'Where I was sure it must be. I'll make the whole matter clear to you soon. I think, Colonel, that you and Watson can return home now and I'll be with you again in an hour at the most. The inspector and I must have a word with the prisoners, but you will certainly see me back at lunchtime.'

I looked forward, as I always did, to the explanation of his deductions. Holmes was as good as his word. At about one o'clock he joined us in the colonel's sitting room. He was accompanied by a little elderly gentleman, who was introduced to me as Mr Acton, the man whose house had been the scene of the original burglary.

'I wished Mr Acton to be present while I explained the matter to you,' said Homes,' for it is natural that he should take a keen interest in the details.

I'm afraid, my dear Colonel, that you must regret ever inviting such a troublemaker as I.'

'On the contrary,' answered the colonel warmly, 'I consider it the greatest privilege to have been permitted to study your methods of working. I confess that they are greater than I expected and I am utterly unable to understand your results. I have not seen a single clue.'

'I'm afraid that my explanation

may disappoint you, but it has always been my habit not to hide any of my methods, either from my friend, Watson, or from anyone who might take an intelligent interest in them. But first, as I am rather shaken by the knocking about that I had in the dressing room, I think that I shall help myself to a dash of your brandy, Colonel. My strength has been rather tested lately.'

'I trust you had no more of

those nervous attacks?'

Holmes laughed heartily.

'We will come to that in a minute,' he said. 'I will explain the case in due course, showing you the various points that guided me in my deductions. Please interrupt me if there are any points that are not clear to you.'

I relaxed in my chair, eagerly awaiting his story.

'One of the most important points in the art of detection is to recognise which facts are important and which are not. Otherwise your energy will be used up on distractions instead of being concentrated on the vital points. Now, in this case, there was not the slightest doubt in my mind right from the start that the key to the whole matter was the scrap of paper in the dead man's hand.

'Before going into this, I draw your attention to this fact. If Alec Cunningham's story was correct, and if the thief, after shooting William Kirwan, had *instantly* fled, then it could not have been he who tore the paper from the dead man's hand. But if it was not he, it must have been Alec Cunningham himself, for by the time the old man had come down several of the staff were at the scene.

'The point is a simple one, but

the inspector had overlooked it because he had assumed that these country gentlemen could have nothing to do with it. Now, I make a point of never having any prejudices and of following wherever the facts lead me.
At the very first stage of the investigation, I queried the part that had been played by Mr Alec Cunningham.

'And now,' went on Holmes, 'I made a very careful examination of the corner of the paper that the inspector had given to us. It

was at once clear to me that it

formed part of a very remarkable

document. Here it is. Do you now

see something very odd about it?'

'It looks very irregular,' said

the colonel.

'My dear

sir,' cried

Holmes, 'there

cannot be the

least doubt in the

world that it has

been written by two

at quarter to twelve
learn what
maybe

people doing alternate words. When I point out the strong t's of "at" and "to", and ask you to compare them with the weak ones of "quarter" and "twelve" you will instantly recognise the fact. A very brief study of these four words would show you that "learn" and the "maybe" are written in the stronger hand, and the "what" in the weaker.'

'Of course! It's as clear as day!' cried the colonel. 'Why on earth should two men write a letter in such a way?'

'It was a dark business and one of the men distrusted the other. He decided that each should have an equal part in it. Now, of the two men, it is clear that the one who wrote "at" and "to" was the ringleader.'

'How do you know that?'

'If you examine this scrap carefully, you can see that

the man with the stronger
handwriting wrote all his
words first, leaving blanks for
the other to fill in. These blank
spaces were not always enough
so that the second man had
to squeeze in his "quarter" in
between the "at" and the "to",
showing that the latter was
already written. The man who
wrote all his words first is
undoubtedly
the man who
planned the deed.'

at   to
learn
maybe

'Excellent!' cried Mr Acton.

'We come now to the point that is important. You may not be aware that in normal cases, experts can now tell a man's age quite accurately from his handwriting. I say normal cases because ill health and physical weakness reproduce the signs of old age, even when the person is young. In this case, looking at the bold, strong writing of the one, and the rather broken-backed appearance of the other, which is still legible even though the 't's' have begun to lose their crossing, we can say that one was a young man and the other much older, although not feeble.'

'Excellent!' cried Mr Acton again.

'There is a further point, however, which is of greater interest,' went on Holmes.

'There is something similar in these two sets of handwriting. They belong to men who are blood relatives. I have no doubt at all that there is a family mannerism in these two specimens of writing. These are only the main results of my examination of the note. There were twenty-three other deductions that would be of more interest to experts than to you. These all tended to make me absolutely certain that the

Cunninghams, father and son,
wrote this letter.

'Having got so far my next
step was, of course, to examine

the details of the crime and see how far they would help us. I went up to the house with the inspector and saw all that was to be seen. The wound on the dead man was, as I was able to tell with absolute confidence, fired from a revolver at a distance of a little over four yards. There was no powder blackening on the clothes, which would have been there if it had been fired at point-blank range. Evidently then, Alec Cunningham had lied when he said that the two men were struggling when the shot was fired. Again, both father and son agreed as to the place where the man escaped into the road. At that place there happens to be a small, damp ditch. As there were no footprints in the ditch, I was absolutely sure that not only had the Cunninghams lied again, but that there had never been any unknown man at the scene at all.'

Mr Acton nodded.

'And now I have to consider

the motive for this strange crime. To get at this, I tried first of all to solve the reason for the original burglary at Mr Acton's. I understood from the colonel that there had been a court case going on between you and the Cunninghams, Mr Acton. It instantly occurred to me that they had broken into your library with the intention of getting at some document that might be of importance in the case.'

'Precisely so,' said Mr Acton.

'There can be no doubt about their intentions. I have the clearest claim upon half of their present estate and if they could have found a single paper – which fortunately was in a safe at my solicitor's – they would undoubtedly have ruined our case.'

'There you are,' said Holmes, smiling. 'It was a dangerous, reckless attempt that I traced to young Alec. Having found no documents, they made it look like an ordinary burglary and took anything they could get. What I really wanted was to get hold of the missing part of the note. I was certain that Alec had torn it from the dead man's hand, and almost certain that he must have thrust it into the pocket of his dressing gown. Where else could he have put it? The only question was whether it was still there.

It was worth an effort to find out, and that is why we all went up to the house.'

'The Cunninghams joined us outside the kitchen door, as you remember. It was very important that they should not be reminded of the note, otherwise they would have destroyed it straightaway. The inspector was about to remind them of its importance when, by a lucky chance, I fell down in a sort of fit and so changed their conversation.'

'Good heavens!' cried the colonel, laughing. 'Do you mean to say that all our sympathy was wasted and you weren't ill at all?'

'Speaking as a doctor, it was very well done!' I said, looking in amazement at this man who was forever surprising

me with some new aspect of his cleverness.

'It is an art that is often useful,' he said. 'When I recovered I managed very ingeniously to get old Cunningham to write the word "twelve", so that I could compare it with the "twelve" on the paper.'

'Oh, what an idiot I have been!' I exclaimed, remembering Holmes' error with the time on the reward advertisement.

'I could see that you were

sympathising with me over my weakness,' said Holmes, laughing. 'I was sorry to cause you the anxiety that I know you felt. We then went upstairs together. Having entered Alec's room and seen a dressing gown hanging behind the door, I upset a table to distract the Cunninghams for a moment so that I could slip away and examine the pockets. The paper was in one of them as I had expected, but I had hardly got it when the two men were on me. I believe they would have murdered me then and there if it hadn't been for your prompt and friendly aid. As it is, I can feel the young man's grip on my throat now, and the father has twisted my wrist round in an effort to get the paper out of my hand. They saw that I knew all about it, you see, and the sudden change from absolute security to complete despair made them desperate.'

I nodded, marvelling again at

how well he had fooled everyone when he blamed me for the upset table and subsequent mess on the floor. I should have known there was a reason for everything that Holmes did. Nothing was an accident.

'I had a little talk with Cunningham afterwards as to the motive of the crime,' went on Holmes. 'He was calm enough, although his son was a perfect demon, ready to kill himself or anyone else if he could have got to his revolver. When old Cunningham saw that he was beaten he lost all heart and admitted everything. It seems that William had secretly followed his employers on the night when they made their raid on Acton's. Then, having got them in his power, he threatened to report them to the police, and blackmailed them. Mr Alec, however, was a dangerous man with whom to play games. It was a stroke of genius on his part to use the local burglary scare as an opportunity of getting rid of the man whom he feared. William was lured out and shot, and had they got the whole of the note, it's very possible that suspicion would not have been aroused.'

'And the note?' I asked.

Holmes placed the two pieces
of paper in front of us.

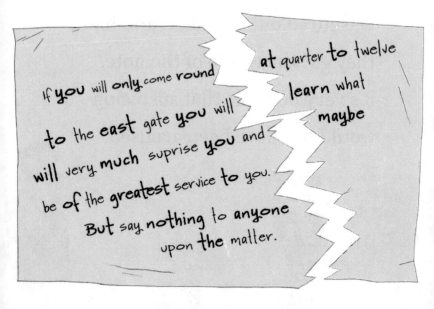

If you will only come round
to the east gate you will
will very much suprise you and
be of the greatest service to you.
But say nothing to anyone
upon the matter.

at quarter to twelve
learn what
maybe

'It's very much the sort of
thing that I expected,' he said.
'Of course, we do not yet know

what William Kirwan expected to learn. But the trap was skilfully baited.'

'Watson, I think our quiet rest in the country has been a distinct success, and I shall certainly return much invigorated to Baker Street tomorrow.'

I looked at his cheerful face and could only agree that the investigation had done him the world of good.

Sherlock Holmes

World-renowned private detective Sherlock Holmes has solved hundreds of mysteries, and is the author of such fascinating monographs as *Early English Charters* and *The Influence of a Trade Upon the Form of a Hand*. He keeps bees in his free time.

Dr John Watson

Wounded in action at Marwan, Dr John Watson left the army and moved into 221B Baker Street. There he was surprised to learn that his new friend, Sherlock Holmes, faced daily peril solving crimes, and began documenting his investigations.
Dr Watson also runs a doctor's practice.

To download Sherlock Holmes activities, please visit www.sweetcherrypublishing.com/resources